KiND KEN

Being kind feels so good

DOROTHY HARVEY

To order additional copies of this book, contact:
Xlibris
844-714-8691
www.Xlibris.com
Orders@Xlibris.com

ISBN: Softcover   978-1-6698-1325-5
        EBook   978-1-6698-1324-8

Print information available on the last page

Rev. date: 02/21/2022

"Animal lover, animal lover!" someone shouted from behind the trees.

Ken knew just who that was. It was Billy, the bully from school.

Ken ignored him and just kept on walking.

Ken was an eight-year-old boy who lived with his mom, dad, and baby sister. He adored his sister, Ann. Ann, was two years old. She enjoyed playing with her big brother. At nighttime, he read a bedtime story to her. She always looked forward to hearing him read one of her favorite stories.

Ken enjoyed playing with small animals. They loved Ken and sometimes followed him to school. One day when Ken was on his way to school, some kids were throwing stones at a frog, but Ken sheltered the frog. He grabbed it up quickly and gently hid it inside his pocket.

He then continued on his way to school.

Just as the students were completing a class test, there was a loud noise.

"Ribbit." Everyone's attention went into the direction of Ken.

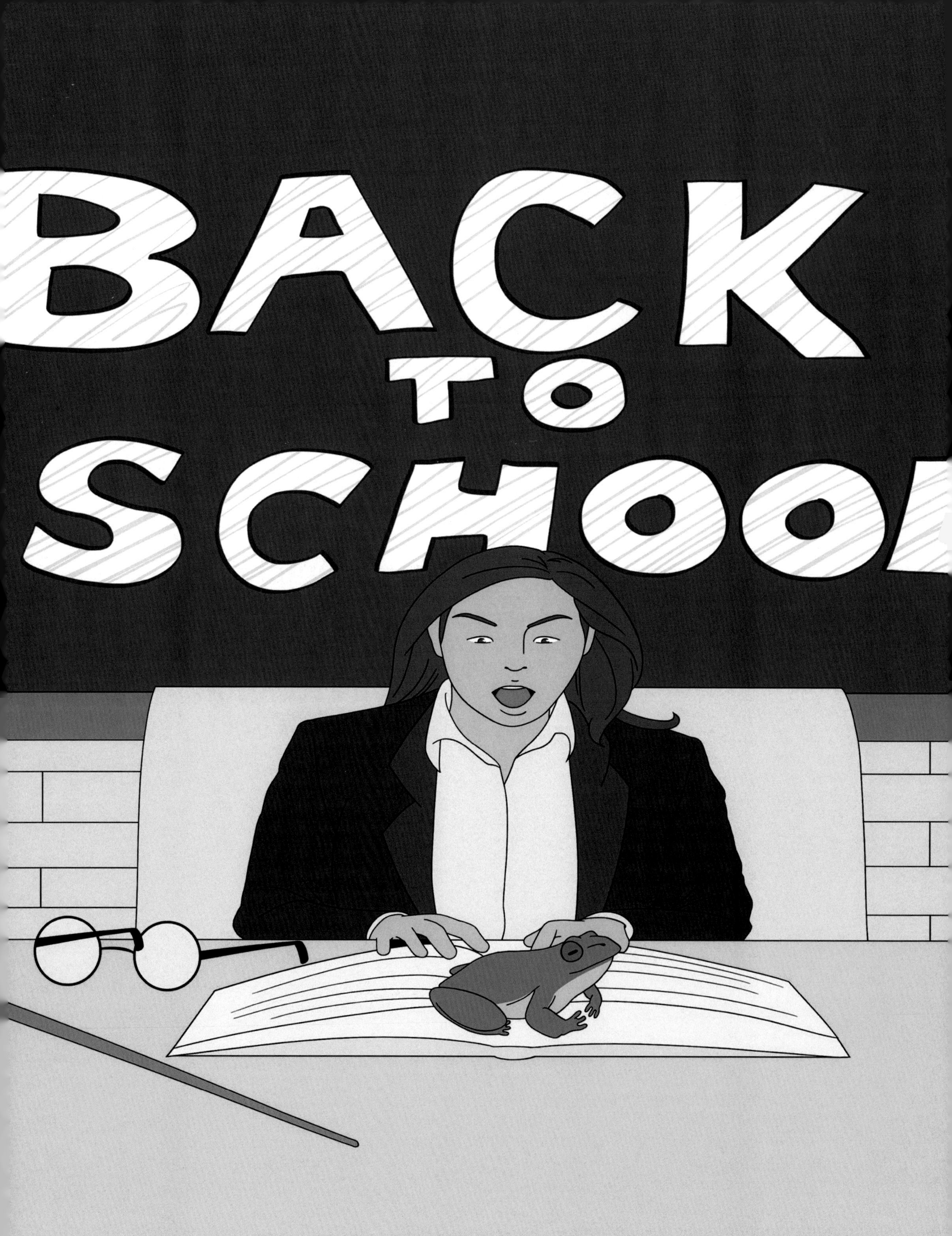
BACK TO SCHOO

"Ribbit... Ribbit." The frog jumped from Ken's shirt pocket and landed with a splash on his desk. The girls were screaming and the boys were laughing.

Mrs. Butler, the teacher, was furious.

"Who brought this frog into my classroom?" she shouted. Just then the frog landed on her desk.

Ken rushed up to the front of the classroom and caught the frog and ran outside with it.

Several days later, when Ken was on his way home from school, he saw a baby lizard in the street. Ken knew that the busy road was an unsafe place, so he tried to catch the baby lizard. When Ken approached the lizard, it ran away because it thought Ken wanted to play. Ken tried to follow, but he slipped and fell into the nearby ditch.

He tried and tried to get out, but without success.

After some time, he shouted, "Help, help, somebody, please help me."

Mama lizard heard the cry for help and came out to see what was happening.

She went over to where the sound was coming from and saw Ken in the ditch. "Ken, I will help you, just a minute." Mama was too small, so she needed to find a way to help Ken.

She then remembered an old trick that her grandpa taught her when she was little. "1, 2, 3", she counted and then took in a big breath of air.

She got bigger and bigger and bigger until she was huge and strong.

She then lowered her big tail into the ditch. "Hold on to my tail, Ken, and I will pull you up."

Ken quickly held on to Mama Lizard's tail, and she started pulling him up. Slowly she pulled, and slowly Ken started to come out of the ditch, but she got too tired to continue.

Right then, Papa Lizard came out to see what Mama was doing. When he saw how big she was, he knew that she needed his help. "1, 2, 3", he counted and then took in a big breath of air.

He got bigger and bigger and bigger
until he was huge and strong.

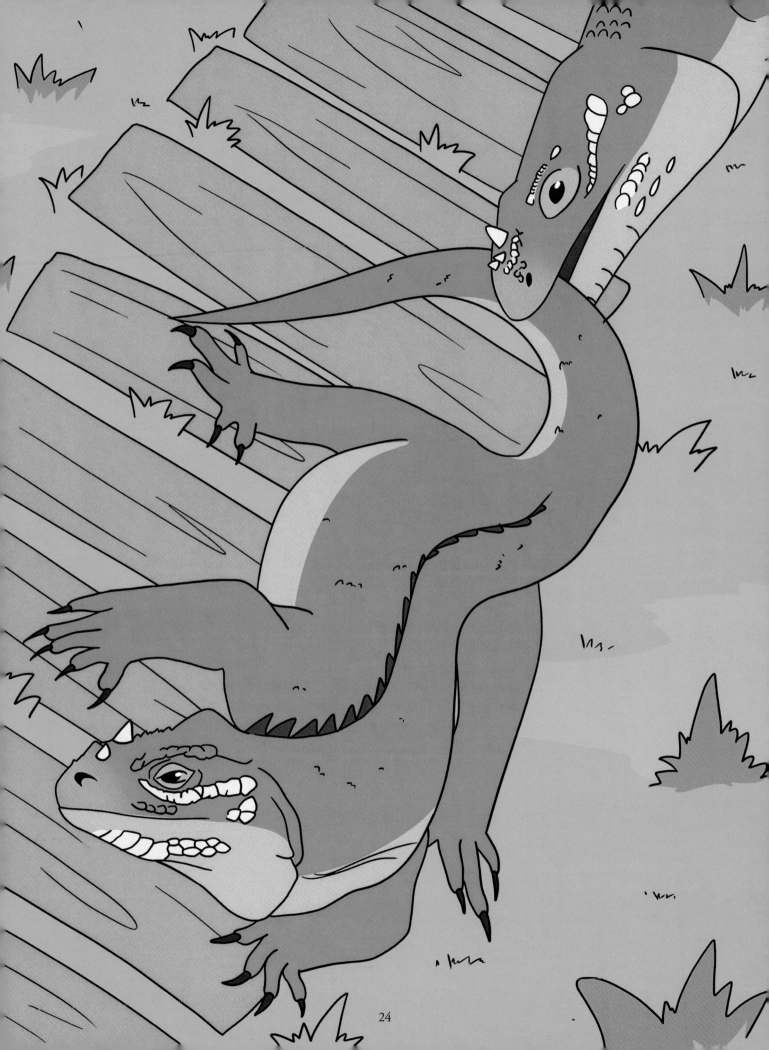

He then called out to Mama Lizard. "Hold on to my tail, Mama, and I will help you pull him up."

"Hold on, Ken, we will pull you up," Mama said to Ken.

Papa pulled, and Mama pulled. Papa pulled, and Mama pulled until Ken was out of the ditch.

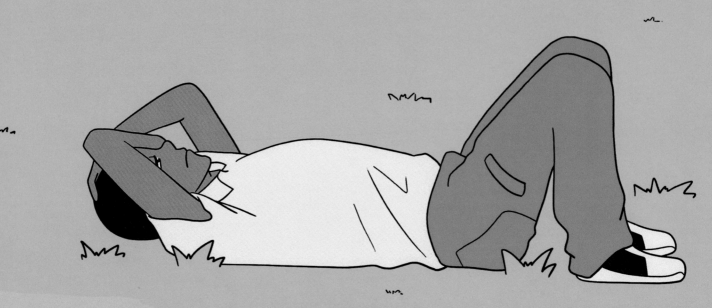

They were extremely tired, so
they all rested on the grass.

Ken was very thankful for their help, so he told them, "Thanks very much for being so kind to me." He then took the baby lizard out of his shirt pocket and gave it to Mama Lizard.

She told Ken that he was the kindest person she knew and was happy she could repay his kindness by helping him that day.

They waved bye to Ken and happily went home.

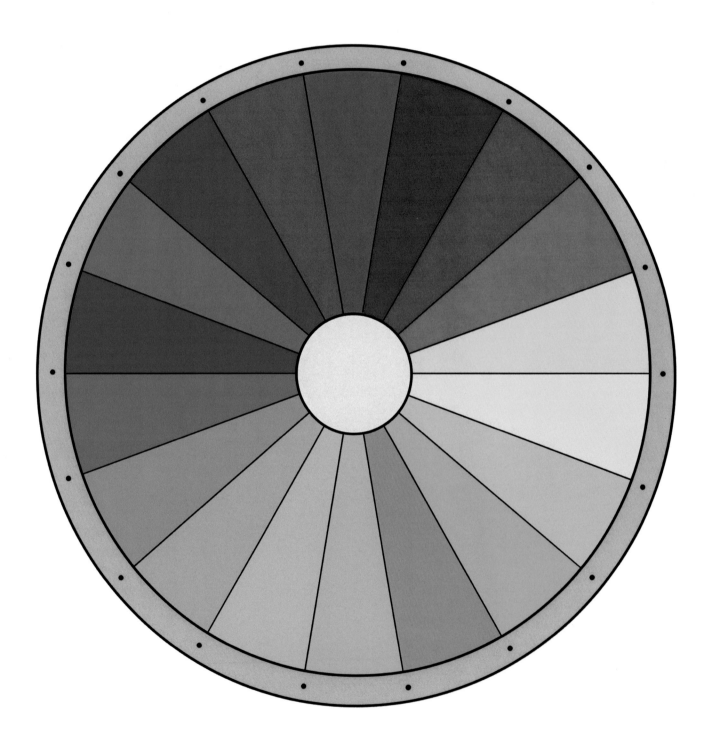

Kindness is like a wheel.

It rolls round and round and round.

Keep giving, and you will never be in need!

Printed in the United States
by Baker & Taylor Publisher Services